For my wonderful sister Swapna, who is courageous,
beautiful, and brilliant—all my love
SP-H

To Katie, Benny, and George
DL

Inspired by Psalm 30:5—*"Weeping may tarry for the night,*
but joy comes with the morning."

Text copyright © 2020 by Smriti Prasadam-Halls
Illustrations copyright © 2020 by David Litchfield

First US edition 2020

Library of Congress Catalog Card Number pending
ISBN 978-1-5362-1283-9

CCP 25 24 23 22 21 20
10 9 8 7 6 5 4 3 2

Printed in Shenzhen, Guangdong, China

This book was typeset in Bentham.
The illustrations were done in ink and paint and rendered digitally.

Candlewick Press
99 Dover Street
Somerville, Massachusetts 02144

www.candlewick.com

RAIN BEFORE
Rainbows

Smriti Prasadam-Halls

illustrated by
David Litchfield

CANDLEWICK PRESS

Rain before rainbows.

Clouds before sun.

Night before daybreak.

The old day is done.

There are mountains for climbing.

Journeys to take.

Dreams that are hopeful. Decisions to make.

Dark days may shake us and worries creep in,

with dragons to duel and battles to win.

Thunder will rumble. Lightning will flash.
The wind will start blowing, and tall waves will crash.

But . . . there are footsteps to follow and words that are wise.

There's a map that will guide us when troubles arise.

There are friends who will help us, courageous and kind.

A rope to hold on to . . .

and treasure to find.

Sowing and planting.

Roots before shoot.

Stem before flower.

Leaf before fruit.

Rain before rainbows, clouds before sun,
night before daybreak—a new day's begun.

A day full of promise, a day full of light ...
The morning is breaking ...

and the morning is bright.